UMM KULTHUM

THE STAR OF THE EAST

by Rhonda Roumani
illustrated by Ahmed Abdelmohsen

Crocodile Books, USA
An imprint of Interlink Publishing Group, Inc.

To Samia: May your star always shine bright and your voice always ring clear.

In the small village of Tammay on the Nile Delta in Egypt, the cries of a newborn baby pierced the crisp morning air. A midwife stepped out of a mud-brick home to announce the birth of a healthy baby. When she neglected to mention whether the baby was a boy or a girl, the father, the village sheikh, smiled.

He immediately knew his wife had delivered a baby girl. Back then, people preferred boys to girls. But Sheikh Ibrahim was a pious man who loved all of God's creations.

"We will call our daughter Umm Kulthum," Sheikh Ibrahim announced happily to all.

Umm Kulthum was an unusual name for a baby. The sheikh's family begged him to change it to something more popular. But the sheikh refused. He wanted a serious name for his little girl. And what could be more honorable than the name of one of the Prophet's daughters?

Umm Kulthum was born at a time when people rode carriages; before water ran through pipes or electricity lit up homes; before people communicated by telephone. It was a time when few girls went to school and certainly did not sing in public.

But just like her name, Umm Kulthum was no ordinary girl.

Every morning, Umm Kulthum watched her older brother Khaled prepare his books for the *kuttab*, the religious school children attended in the countryside.

She begged her parents to let her go, too.

Umm Kulthum's father did not know where he would find the extra money to send his daughter to school. But Umm Kulthum wouldn't take no for an answer. At the *kuttab*, she learned to recite the Qur'an by heart.

She became one of the few girls from her village to learn to read and write.

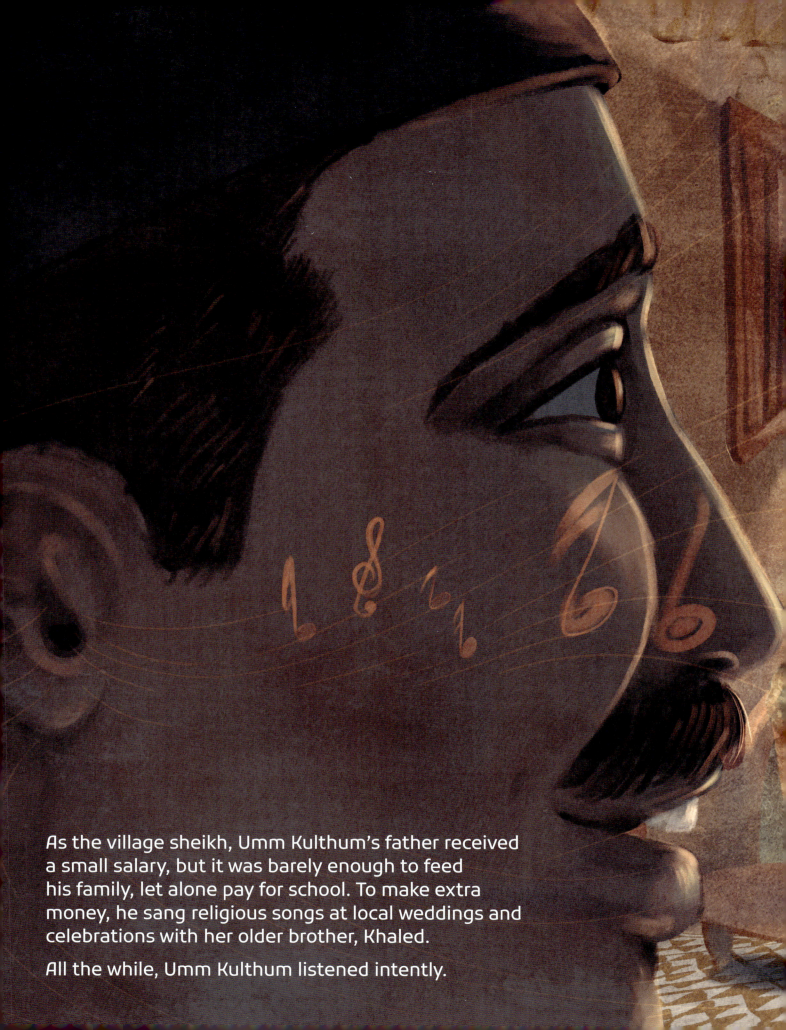

As the village sheikh, Umm Kulthum's father received a small salary, but it was barely enough to feed his family, let alone pay for school. To make extra money, he sang religious songs at local weddings and celebrations with her older brother, Khaled.

All the while, Umm Kulthum listened intently.

In secret, Umm Kulthum sang the same rhythmic chants to her rag doll, which her grandmother had made from scraps of cloth and a lock of her own hair.

One morning, her father overheard Umm Kulthum. He couldn't believe his ears. Her voice was strong and confident; her pronunciation nearly perfect. From that day on, Umm Kulthum joined her brother and father in all their rehearsals.

One day, her father asked Umm Kulthum to sing with them at a *mawlid*, a celebration of the Prophet Muhammad's birthday, at the home of the village chief. Umm Kulthum refused. She liked singing to her doll, but she did not want to sing in public. Her father offered her candy, but, again, she said no. Then, he offered her a bowl of her favorite dessert: a milky, creamy, heavenly pudding called *muhalabiyah*.

Umm Kulthum couldn't resist.

At the *mawlid*, Sheikh Ibrahim asked Umm Kulthum to sit next to him on a wooden bench and sing. Instead, she hopped up onto the bench, tall and proud, and sang, just like she did when she sang to her doll.

From then on, Umm Kulthum joined her father and brother in all of their performances. And after each performance, Umm Kulthum enjoyed a yummy bowl of *muhalabiyah*.

Over the next few years, Umm Kulthum traveled the Egyptian countryside with her father, singing the praises of Allah and the Prophet Muhammad at tented festivals and the homes of village leaders.

Sometimes they walked for hours over dusty roads in the sweltering heat, only to make the same trek home at the end of the night. It was exhausting. But Umm Kulthum loved visiting the different villages and cities along the Nile. She even took her small cat with her for company.

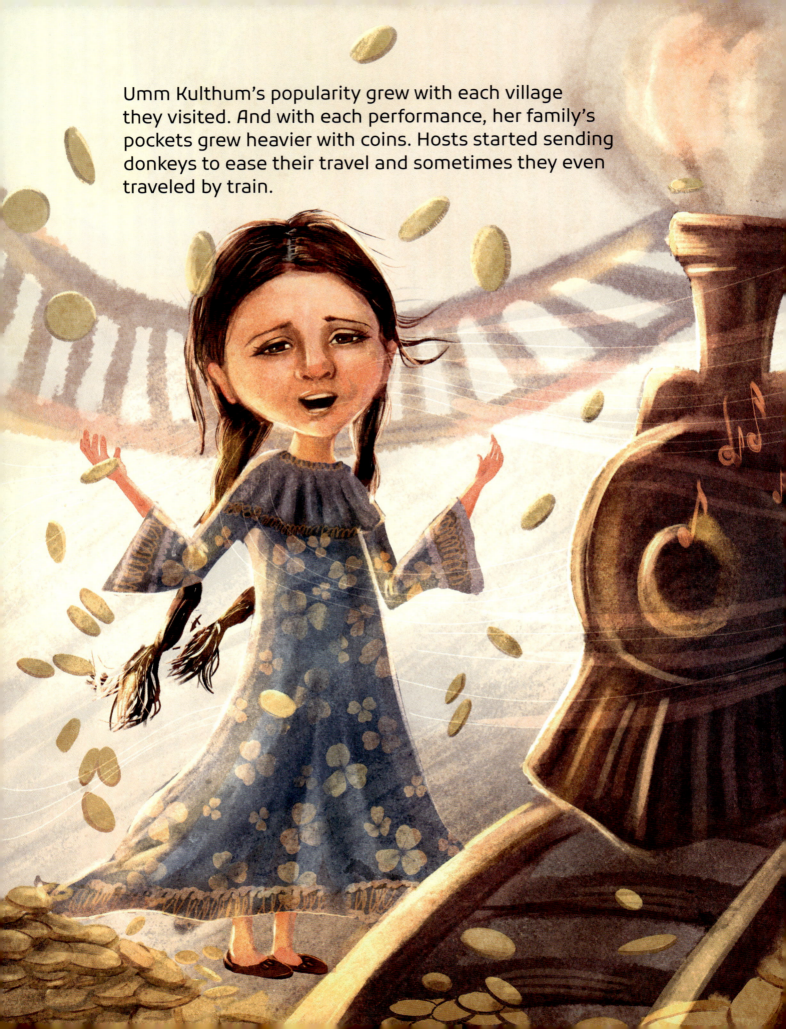

Umm Kulthum's popularity grew with each village they visited. And with each performance, her family's pockets grew heavier with coins. Hosts started sending donkeys to ease their travel and sometimes they even traveled by train.

Umm Kulthum was happy. Her father no longer worried about money, or whether they could afford food or new clothes for Eid.

In just a few years, Umm Kulthum had become known across the Egyptian countryside as the little girl with the powerful voice.

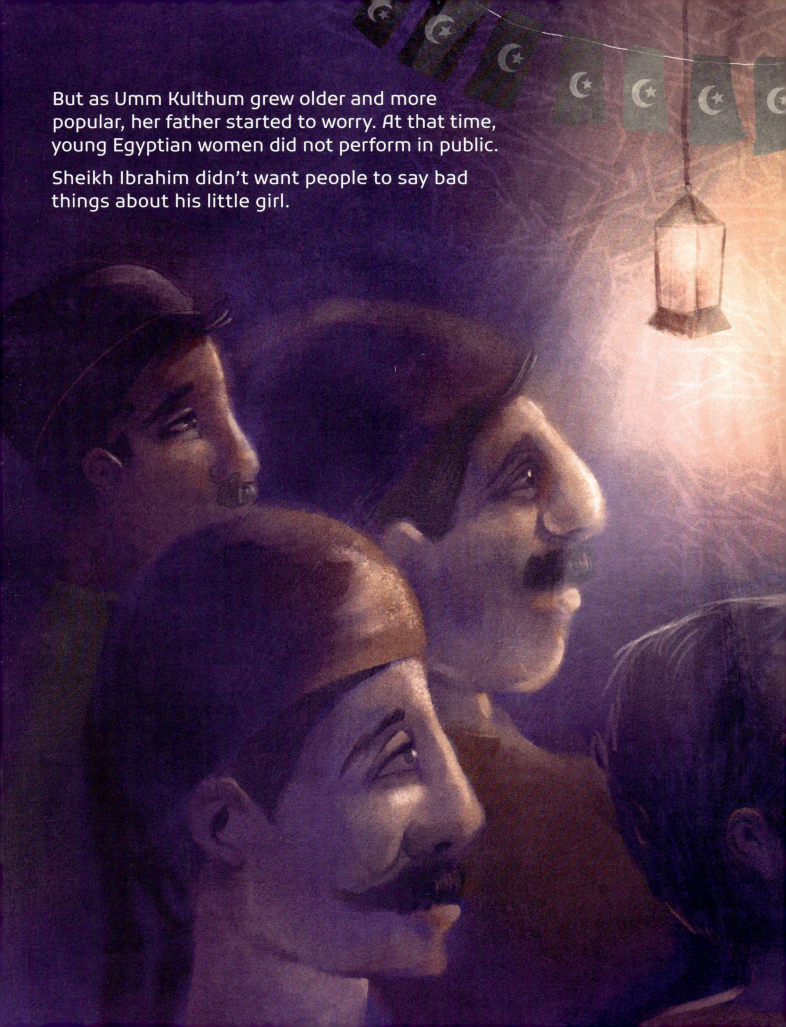

But as Umm Kulthum grew older and more popular, her father started to worry. At that time, young Egyptian women did not perform in public.

Sheikh Ibrahim didn't want people to say bad things about his little girl.

To avoid criticism, Umm Kulthum's father dressed her like a boy. She wore a *gallabiyah*, a long gown worn by men, with a *zibun*, a long vest, and a *kuffiyah* and *'igal*, a headdress with a black cord that kept it in place. Umm Kulthum dressed like this for several years whenever she sang in public.

When Umm Kulthum was a teenager, she heard the most beautiful voice playing on a record player at the house of the village mayor. The voice belonged to Sheikh Aboulela, who sang beautiful lines of Arabic poetry in a traditional style.

At that moment, Umm Kulthum felt like this man was singing only to her.

Right then, she realized what had been missing from her own performances. She sang the right words and the right notes. But she did not always understand the meaning of the words she sang. Umm Kulthum resolved, right then and there, to never sing another word or note that she didn't understand.

Umm Kulthum carefully studied Sheikh Aboulela's recordings. Then, one day, Umm Kulthum spotted the sheikh at a train station near her home. She couldn't believe it! She begged her father to invite him to lunch. A few hours later, she was seated next to the man with the magnificent voice, singing along with him.

They sang together for hours. When they finished, Sheikh Aboulela told Umm Kulthum's father that they must move to Cairo, the capital of Egypt.

"The future of your daughter is much grander than the village of Tammay," he told Sheikh Ibrahim.

"It's a shame to imprison her great talent in such a small village."
Umm Kulthum's father refused. He did not want to leave their village. And he worried about his daughter becoming a professional singer. But, at that moment, Umm Kulthum knew her future awaited her in Cairo.

Slowly, over weeks and months, she pressed her father to reconsider. Friends and musicians also tried to persuade him.

One day, he finally agreed to move.

To Umm Kulthum, Cairo felt like another planet...

It was busy, bustling, and bursting with crowds. Cars filled the streets, alongside horse-drawn carriages. Tall, fancy buildings lined wide avenues. British officers roamed the streets and elegant women threw elaborate parties. And a new type of music, with foreign instruments and new tempos and lyrics, filled Cairo's music halls.

What Umm Kulthum didn't know was that Cairo was in the midst of change. A few years earlier, Egyptians had revolted against the British, who controlled their country. The revolution had not succeeded, but Egyptians were tired of being ruled by outsiders.

In Cairo, thinkers, writers, and musicians were busy debating the Western music and ideas that filled their coffee houses and music halls.

Meanwhile, Umm Kulthum performed in the palaces of the wealthiest and most influential people in Cairo, where she encountered riches unlike anything she had ever seen.

She sang in rowdy, crowded music halls in the Azbakiyya Gardens district of Cairo, where dancers, musicians, actors, and singers entertained boisterous crowds late into the night.

It was a far cry from the religious festivals and village gatherings that she was used to. But night after night, Umm Kulthum sang and sang.

When she performed her religious songs, the crowds booed. They wanted the modern, flirty love songs that were popular at the time. Journalists made fun of the peasant girl who wore cheap cotton clothes, and who sang with sheikhs instead of a professional band. They called her simple. Old-fashioned. And unsophisticated. They even spread false rumors about her in the newspaper, which made her father furious.

But Umm Kulthum was determined. She tried singing the popular love songs, but those didn't feel right to her.

She wanted people to love the classical Egyptian music she had grown up singing. So she worked even harder. She sang for hours with Sheikh Aboulela, who helped her control her powerful voice.

She even learned to play the oud and read poetry so she could better connect to the music she was singing.

One day, Umm Kulthum met a famous young poet named Ahmed Rami. Ahmed loved Umm Kulthum's voice so much that he wrote poems for her to sing. His poems were about Egypt and the Nile, about love, longing, and freedom. They were perfect.

Famous composers put the lyrics to music, and professional musicians accompanied her. She even traded in her *gallabiya* for long, luxurious gowns that still reflected her traditional ways.

Umm Kulthum performed music with notes, tones, and scales that were familiar to Egyptian ears. Soon after, she released her first album, which sold millions of copies. Over the course of a single decade, she had transformed from a simple village girl to the most famous singer in Egypt.

The most important poets and musicians in Egypt and the Arab world wrote lyrics and composed music for Umm Kulthum. Record companies competed for her contracts.

She held sold-out concerts that ran late into the night. Audiences swooned as she sang songs that lasted more than an hour. They even called for encores of individual lines. Some say she never repeated the lines the same way twice.

For over forty years, on the first Thursday of every month, Umm Kulthum broadcast a monthly concert on Egyptian Radio. Across the Arab world—from Rabat to Baghdad and Aleppo to Sana'a—shops closed and streets emptied, as millions of listeners rushed home to tune in to her concerts, which lasted for several hours.

Over time, she became the most famous Arab singer in the world. She recorded more than 300 songs during her lifetime and performed in all the major capitals in the Middle East. She starred in films and even became a fashion icon, known for wearing dark, cat-eye sunglasses indoors and carrying a handkerchief whenever she sang.

Her music transformed to meet the needs of the time. When Egypt and the Arab world went to war with its colonial powers, she sang songs about their glory. In 1967, Umm Kulthum toured to raise money for the war effort.

During that tour, she held her only European concert at the famous Olympia Theater in Paris, France. When a journalist asked Umm Kulthum, "What was the most beautiful place you saw while in Paris?"

Umm Kulthum quickly responded, "The obelisk," referring to an ancient Egyptian obelisk that stands in the center of Paris. When asked why, she said simply: "Because it's ours."

Decades later, Umm Kulthum's music can still be heard in taxis, cafés, and homes across the Arabic-speaking world. Over the course of more than a century, her success has earned her many nicknames: *Al-Sit* (The Lady), *Al Haram al-Rabe'* (Egypt's Fourth Pyramid), and even, *Umm al-Arab* (Mother of the Arabs).

The Arab world couldn't help but fall in love with the Egyptian woman with the powerful voice, who sang their story and reclaimed their history.

She would be forever known as the village girl who became the *Kawkab al-Sharq* (The Star of the East).

Author's Note & Acknowledgments

Some of my earliest memories as a Syrian-American growing up in southern California are of family friends, singing and dancing to the songs of famous Arab singers. Although Umm Kulthum made the occasional appearance, it wasn't until I was in high school that she really entered our lives.

In the 1990s, my father, a Syrian urologist from Damascus, befriended Ahmed Zewail, an Egyptian scientist from Cairo. (Many years later, Amo Ahmed, as we called him, would go on to win the Nobel Prize in Chemistry.) Music was one of the things that bonded them. From an early age, my father had developed a love of classical music. Every weekend, Beethoven, Mozart, Wagner, and Puccini blared from his basement office, rattling the entire house.

But soon, when Amo Ahmed would visit, a new voice started emerging out of my father's basement, deep and powerful. Amo Ahmed loved Umm Kulthum. When her music played, he would sit back, close his eyes, and breathe in her voice and words. To me, he looked like he had traveled thousands of miles away from Pasadena and landed back home, on the shores of Alexandria, Egypt.

For a kid who learned Arabic growing up in the US, Umm Kulthum's lyrics were more difficult to access than, say, the light, airy music of Lebanon's Fairuz. Plus, a single song could last for almost an hour. But the more I listened to her voice and learned about Egypt, the more fascinated I became with music and her story.

Umm Kulthum was more than just an artist. She was a poor girl from a village in Egypt, the daughter of a sheikh, who became an Arab icon. People took pride in her perfect pronunciation of the Arabic language, which they attributed to her knowledge of the Qur'an. Her vocal range was legendary, and her voice was so strong she often sang without a microphone. When Umm Kulthum passed away on February 3, 1975, millions of Egyptians flooded the streets to mourn. Nearly five decades after her death, Umm Kulthum is still considered the most famous singer in the Arab world.

During her lifetime, Umm Kulthum gave very few interviews. In telling her story, I relied heavily on her own words whenever possible and on an interview she gave to Egyptian journalist Mahmud 'Awad, translated in a book titled *Middle Eastern Muslim Women Speak* by Elizabeth Warnock Fernea and Basima Qattan Bezirgan.

My sincere and eternal gratitude to Virginia Danielson, the biographer of Umm Kulthum, who allowed me to interview her several times for this book. Her book *The Voice of Egypt: Umm Kulthum, Arabic Song, and Egyptian Society* was a vital resource for this book.

Arabic Music & Instruments

Arabic music is different from Western music both in its tones and in the types of instruments used. Arabic music has quarter tones, while Western music relies mostly on half tones. This means that between two notes there exist other micro-notes; and, hence, more distinct tones. Arabic music also relies more heavily on melody and rhythm, rather than harmony. The *takht* (literally "platform"), or traditional Arabic ensemble, is made up of five different instruments: the oud, the qanun, the nay, the riq, and the violin, which are each described below.

Oud (or 'ud): The oud is a pear-shaped, fretless, short-necked string instrument with five double courses of strings and one bass string. It is played with a plectrum known as *risha* (Arabic for feather).

Qanun: The qanun is a trapezoid-shaped, zither-type stringed instrument that is played on the player's lap. It is made up of 81 strings that are distributed in 27 rows, with each row consisting of three strings. Each row has the same tone. It is played with a plectrum or pick on the forefinger of each hand.

Nay: Nay means "reed" in Farsi. The nay is an open ended reed flute of varying lengths, which determine the pitch of the instrument. It is a soulful instrument that has nine joints and seven holes: six in the front and one in the back, at the bottom, for the thumb.

Riq: The riq is a small, hand held, tambourine-like percussion instrument. Its frame is made of wood and has five sets of brass cymbals in groups of four.

Violin: The violin was added to the Arabic ensemble in the mid-1800s. Before that time, indigenous stringed instruments such as the *kamanja* (spike fiddle) and the *rababa* were used. Those instruments were played standing, on one's knee. The violin is tuned differently by Middle Eastern musicians in order to produce the distinct tones.

Bibliography

Danielson, Virginia. *The Voice of Egypt: Umm Kulthum, Arabic Song, and Egyptian Society in the Twentieth Century.* The University of Chicago Press, 1997.

Fernea, Elizabeth Warnock and Bezirgan, Basima Qattan. *Middle Eastern Muslim Women Speak.* University of Texas Press, 1977. (Excerpts from "*The Umm Kulthum Nobody Knows,*" as told by Umm Kulthum, famed Egyptian singer, to Mahmud 'Awad, translated by the editors.)

For an extensive bibliography, learning resources, and discography please visit https://www.rhondaroumani.com/books/ummkulthum

First published in 2024 by
Crocodile Books
An imprint of Interlink Publishing Group, Inc.
46 Crosby Street
Northampton, Massachusetts 01060
www.interlinkbooks.com

Text copyright © Rhonda Roumani, 2024
Illustrations copyright © Ahmed Abdelmohsen, 2024
Book design copyright © Interlink Publishing, 2024

All rights reserved. No part of this publication may be reproduced, stored in a retrieval system, or transmitted, in any form or by any means, without the prior written permission of the publisher.

Library of Congress Cataloging-in-Publication Data available
ISBN 978-1-62371-660-8

10 9 8 7 6 5 4 3 2 1
Printed and bound in Korea